First Flight

First Flight

by David McPhail

Scholastic Inc.
New York Toronto London Auckland Sydney
Mexico City New Delhi Hong Kong

for Brecon
and
for Melanie
(After all, it was her idea!)

ISBN 0-439-17979-3

Copyright © 1987 by David McPhail. Published by Scholastic Inc., 555 Broadway,
New York, NY 10012, by arrangement with Little, Brown and Company (Inc.).
SCHOLASTIC and associated logos are trademarks
and/or registered trademarks of Scholastic Inc.

12 11 10 9 8 7 6 5 4 3 21   0 1 2 3 4 5/0

Printed in the U.S.A.

First Scholastic printing, April 2000

I'm going to visit my grandma. I'm going to fly.
It will be my first flight.

My mother and father drive me to the airport.

I get my ticket…

find my gate…

and go through security.

While I'm waiting,
I watch them get my plane ready.

11

When my number is called, I get on the plane.

I find my seat

and put away my suitcase.

I buckle my seat belt and listen to the safety rules.

I sit back and relax while the plane takes off.

I look out the window.

The world below is getting smaller. I think I see my house.

In a little while lunch is served.

After lunch there's a movie.

It's kind of sad...but it has a happy ending.

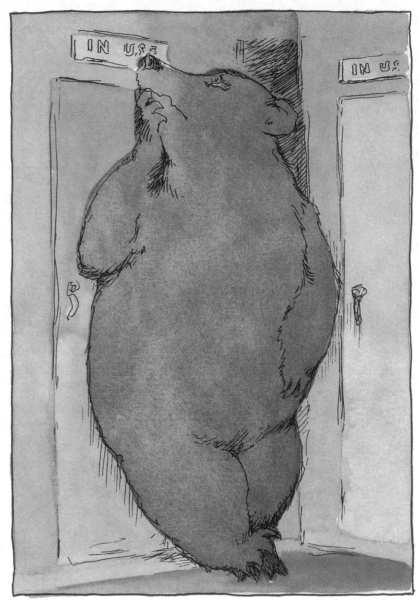

When the movie is over, I go to the bathroom.

The plane begins to bounce. The captain asks us to take our seats.

We are flying through a storm. The plane bounces a lot!

The captain calls it "turbulence."

When the plane stops bouncing, I read my book.

I'm tired. I take a nap.

I wake up when I hear something go "bump."
It is the landing gear. We are coming in for a landing!

I check my seat belt. Almost before I know it, we are on the ground.

When we arrive at the gate, I undo my seat belt and collect my things.

As I'm getting off the plane,
the captain stops me.

He says I was a good passenger.
He gives me some wings just like his.

My grandmother is waiting for me.

"How was your first flight?" she asks.

"Wonderful!" I say, and I tell her all about it.